The Monster
in the
Backpack

The Monster
in the
Backpack

Lisa Moser
illustrated by Noah Z. Jones

CANDLEWICK PRESS
CAMBRIDGE, MASSACHUSETTS

Annie's new backpack came with pink and blue flowers.

Annie's new backpack came with a zipper.

Annie's new backpack came with a monster.

Annie unzipped the backpack and
peeked inside.
"AAAAHHHH!" yelled the monster.

"EEEEEEKKKK!" yelled Annie.
Annie dropped the backpack and jumped
across the sidewalk.

She waited one,

two,

three minutes.

Slowly, slowly she tiptoed across the sidewalk and peeked inside again.

"AAAAHHHH!" yelled the monster.

"Do you ever whisper?" asked Annie.

"Do you ever knock?" asked the monster.

"How can I knock on a backpack?"

The monster scratched his head.
"You're right," he said.
"Next time, ring the doorbell."

"What are you doing in my backpack?"
Annie asked.

"Eating a snack," said the monster,
licking peanut butter off his paws.

"That's not a snack," said Annie.
"That's my sandwich!"
She reached into the backpack and
pulled out some brown squishy things.

"I saved the crusts for you,"
said the monster.

"Yuck," said Annie.
"What else did you save for me?"

"I'll see," said the monster.

He dove into the backpack.

He threw out an empty juice box,

potato-chip crumbs, and a banana peel.

Finally, he popped up with a little bag in his paw. "I don't like carrots," said the monster. "They make me burp."

Annie zipped the monster into the backpack. "I definitely don't need a burping monster."

When Annie got to school, she hung the backpack on her coat hook.

It jumped off.

She hung it up. It jumped off.

On. Off.

On. Off.

On. Off.

"Hold still," Annie whispered.

"I don't like to be alone," the monster whispered back.

"Oh, all right. I don't like to be alone, either." Annie dragged the backpack to her seat and wiggled it under her desk.

At recess, Mrs. Hardy said, "It's been raining. Put on your boots."

Annie pulled and tugged. She tugged and pulled. "My backpack's stuck," said Annie. "My boots are inside."

"Keep trying," said Mrs. Hardy. "We'll wait in the hall."

Annie grabbed the backpack.

She gave a giant tug.

ZING!

Her backpack unzipped.

"You're in big trouble," said Annie.

"Really?" asked the monster.

"Yes. I need my boots, and you were holding the zipper shut."

"Oh, you can't have your right boot," said the monster. "I sleep in it."

"You can't sleep in my boot."

"Why not?" asked the monster. "Does it give me boot-head?"

Annie looked at the monster.
She laughed.
"That's how you always look."

"And you can't have your left boot either,"
said the monster. "It's full of bubble gum."

"Why did you put bubble gum in my boot?"
asked Annie.

"Because I was done chewing it."

Annie pulled gobs of gooey gum out of her boot.

"Give me that boot," said Annie.

"Oh, NO, NO, NO," said the monster.

Suddenly, the monster stopped pulling.

"Put those boots on right away."

"Why?" asked Annie.

"If you wear your boots,
        you'll go outside.
If you go outside,
        you'll run around.
If you run around,
        your boots will get hot and stinky.
If I sleep in those boots,
I'll get stinky, too. I LOVE to be stinky!"

Annie pulled on her boots.
"You're a very strange monster.
Strange, but interesting."

Annie sat next to Kate at the lunch table.
"I like your new backpack," said Kate.

"That backpack is big trouble," said Annie.

"Mine is plain green, but yours is so pretty.
Do you want to trade?" asked Kate.

"I'll think about it," said Annie,
crunching a carrot. Her
hungry tummy rumbled.

After lunch, Mrs. Hardy said, "Take out your homework."

Annie reached into her backpack for her homework. All she found were tiny bits of shredded paper. "Where's my homework?" she whispered.

"I ripped it up," said the monster. "I'm making a surprise."

"You ripped up my homework?
Now I'll have to start all over."

"Don't worry," said the monster.
"I can still work on my surprise."

Annie thought about Kate's backpack.
Green was a nice color.

Suddenly the monster blew a horn.

He jumped up and down.

He threw paper in the air.

Tiny bits of paper flew up Annie's nose.

Tiny bits of paper flew into Annie's ears.

Tiny bits of paper flew into Annie's mouth.

"Now what are you doing?" asked Annie.

"Having a parade!" said the monster.

Mrs. Hardy walked by. "Oh, dear.

You'll have to clean this up."

"Did you love the parade?"
asked the monster.

"No!" said Annie. "I'm really mad!
Look at this mess."

The monster looked at Annie.
A big tear rolled down his cheek.
He blew his nose into Annie's hat.

"Why did you have a parade, anyway?"
asked Annie.

"It was the ANNIE-IS-GREAT PARADE,"
said the monster.

He slid deep down into the backpack
and zipped it shut.

Annie stared at the backpack.

She patted it gently.

Then she laid her cheek against it.

"Thanks," she whispered.

After school, Annie walked home.
Kate ran up to her. "Do you want to trade
backpacks now?" asked Kate.

Annie looked at Kate's green backpack.
"No," she said. "I wouldn't trade my
backpack for anything."

"Why not?" asked Kate.

Annie hugged her backpack tight.
"My backpack is silly and messy
and big trouble. But I love my backpack,"
said Annie. "And everything in it!"

Annie put the backpack on and
skipped down the street.
The backpack bounced up and down.

Tiny bits of paper
floated out
all over
the sidewalk.

For Marty
Your love and encouragement are cherished gifts
L. M.

For my three fantastic siblings:
(in no particular order) Nathan, Emily, and Zoe
N. Z. J.

First paperback edition 2007

The Library of Congress has cataloged the hardcover edition as follows:
Moser, Lisa.
The monster in the backpack / Lisa Moser ; illustrated by Noah Jones. – 1st ed.
p.   cm.
Summary: Annie's new backpack comes with pink and blue flower decorations, a zipper, and a
mischievous monster who manages to get her into all sorts of trouble at school.
ISBN 978-0-7636-2390-6 (hardcover)
[1. Monsters – Fiction. 2. Backpacks – Fiction. 3. Schools – Fiction.]   I. Jones, Noah (Noah Z.), ill.
PZ7.M84696Mon 2006
[Fic] – dc22   2005045391

ISBN 978-0-7636-3307-3 (paperback)

2 4 6 8 10 9 7 5 3 1

Printed in Singapore

This book was typeset in Humana Sans.
The illustrations were created digitally.

Candlewick Press
2067 Massachusetts Avenue
Cambridge, Massachusetts 02140

visit us at www.candlewick.com